REVELATION

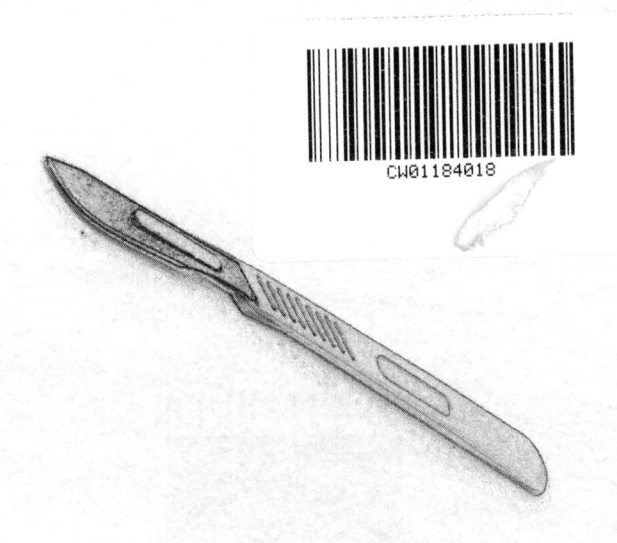

R J Dent

REVELATION

First published by **INCUNABULA** 2024

copyright © **R J Dent**

cover design by **D M Mitchell**

INCUNABULA

www.incunabulamedia.com

ISBN 978-1-4466-0288-1

One

There's neither blame nor guilt on anyone's part for what happened. And even if I were to want to apportion blame, I can't think who the right person to blame would be. But I don't want to point any accusing fingers because at the time everyone had a very lovely time, especially James, my husband. Kristyna, the bride, also enjoyed herself immensely.

As for me, well, I'll leave that for now and start at the start, which I think can be traced back to a warm spring morning when I asked my husband what he wanted for his fifty-fifth birthday.

'You know what I want,' he said, grinning broadly over the arts or the review newspaper supplement he was reading.

I did know what he wanted – he asked for the same thing every year and it had become a running joke – but because I'd decided to give him what he wanted, I decided to be awkward.

'No, I don't know. What?'

'I want to watch you have sex with another woman,' my husband said. 'I have mentioned it once or twice.'

'And what's your second choice?'

'My second choice is I want to watch you have sex with another woman,' my husband said, predictably.

I paused for a few seconds and saw the hope flare up in his eyes.

'And let's just say, hypothetically, that I arranged it, would you just watch? Or would you want to join in?'

I had worded my question carefully and I watched him unwaveringly as he answered.

'I'd just want to watch,' he said, 'but I might want to touch myself... during...'

'I need to know,' I said. 'I need to know exactly what it is you want, what you'll do, how you picture it. So you're going to have to give me every single detail. I don't want any surprises or shocks.'

He nodded.

'Fair enough. I picture it as you and another woman – same age or younger – on our bed, naked and doing things, and I sit at the foot of the bed and watch you.'

'Are you naked?'

He shrugged.

'I don't know. Probably.'

'And would you want to touch... us, me... her?'

'I've not thought of that,' he said. 'What's your thinking on that?'

'I don't want you to touch her at all – whoever 'she' is. In fact, I don't want you to ever touch another woman. Not even one that I've got naked on our bed. I can't begin to tell you how important that is to me. I need you to know that it would end everything between us for me if you ever touched another woman.'

'But I can watch?'

'If I can arrange it, you can watch.'

'Are you going to try and arrange it?'

I nodded slowly.

'Yes, I am. And that's the key word: 'try'. I'm going to *try* to arrange it, but I may not be able to. I don't know how one goes about such things. So it may not happen. If so, then it won't be due to lack of effort on my part.'

I paused for a moment, gathering my thoughts.

'But just so you know, so that there is no doubt, so there are no grey areas, if I *do* arrange it, it'll be a one-off, a once-in-a-lifetime experience, a fifty-fifth birthday present to you from me and one that I won't want to ever refer to or discuss with you afterwards. If you can agree to that, then we have an agreement.'

My husband didn't hesitate.

'I agree to it,' he said.

'I thought you might. You're going to have to give me a list of what you want us to do.'

He nodded.

'I've already written it.'

'Of course you have. Probably more than once too.'

He nodded again and grinned in a mock-sorry way.

I reached out and took his hand and looked at him, suddenly very serious.

'I mean it,' I said. 'If it happens, you can't touch her, nor can you talk about her afterwards. Not ever.'

He squeezed my hand gently.

'I know. I don't want to touch anyone but you. And if it happens, it'll be fantastic, and I'll always remember what you'll have done for me, but I won't talk about her or about it afterwards, I promise.'

I could see he meant it.

'In that case,' I said, 'I'll see what I can do. Go and get your list.'

Two

I did see what I could do, but it took quite a while before I started getting anywhere near anything that could be termed a result. The main problem was that I didn't know how to go about organising such a thing.

Eventually, once I decided to look at escort services, I started to make some headway. No, that was not an intended pun. I made a few discrete enquiries, pretending that I was trying to arrange a lesbian sex show for a man's birthday, which was true, so my level of pretence merely involved not mentioning that I was going to be involved, and not making any reference to the fact that the man it was for was my husband. Some things need to remain unsaid if one is to succeed.

It was fortuitous that I had nearly a year to arrange what I had come to regard as a husband treat. That's what I called it whenever he asked me about it. I'd simply say: 'Your husband treat request is being processed. No more questions.'

And I had a breakthrough when I met one of the escorts. I thought that was the best thing to do. I contacted an escort agency, told them I wanted a lesbian encounter with a young blonde woman and the woman on the phone asked me for some details, including the date on which I wanted my experience. I asked for it to be in two days' time and then I was given the name of a hotel and told to meet 'Kristyna' in the lobby. She spelled the name out carefully. She informed me that Kristyna was Russian.

'You'll make all the arrangements with her,' the woman said. 'She'll greet you like you're an old friend, so don't be surprised. Just go along with it.'

I agreed to everything.

And so I met Kristyna.

Three

The initial meeting itself was fairly innocuous.

I had dressed carefully for the occasion, and for some reason, I was acutely aware of this as I walked into the hotel and looked around the lobby for a young blonde woman. I quickly saw that no one matching that description was there.

At the end of the lobby was a bar so I made my way to it, sat down on a long-legged metal stool and ordered a soda water. Once I had my drink I turned around on my stool so I could see the lobby. I knew it was her the moment she walked in. She was tall and slim, with a square face and attractive features, and her hair was blonde and long and held back in a pony tail. She was wearing a demurely cut dress and sensible shoes. No deliberate flaunting of her looks or her body. No indication of what she did for a living. Blended conventionality; the perfect disguise.

She saw me and gave me more than a cursory glance, so I waved and she walked towards me, a huge smile on her face.

'There you are,' she said excitedly. 'How have you been?'

'Very well, thank you,' I said, enjoying the charade. 'And you?'

'I am okay, thank you' she said, and it was at this point I heard her distinct Russian accent.

I got her a drink – she wanted white wine, and she asked for it to be sent to her room. She gave the room number and the barman gave a bottle and glasses to a waiter who took it away with him somewhere.

'That'll be in your room for you when you go up, madam,' the barman informed her.

She nodded.

'Thank you.'

She asked me how my family was and I answered mechanically, cheerfully, sipping my tonic water until it had gone.

'Shall we go up?'

I nodded and we went up.

Four

In her room, which was a big, well-appointed room, I sat opposite her in a leather wing chair. I sat upright, trying to convey dignity. Kristyna lounged carelessly in her chair, but she somehow managed to look elegant.

The wine was open in an ice bucket on a stand nearby. The glasses were on the low table. They had napkins in them. I removed the napkins and poured us both a glass of chilled white wine. Kristyna leaned forward and picked up her glass. She held it out. I picked up mine and we clinked glasses, toasting something intangible.

We both sat back and sipped our drinks.

'How long would you like?' she asked. 'One hour, two, or all night?'

'I'd like an hour of your time, please,' I said. 'And I'd like to talk to you, because I have a proposition for you. But it's not for me, it's for my husband.'

She fixed her gaze on me and suddenly I could see the core of steel that was inside her.

'Talking or fucking – it costs the same,' she said curtly.

'Of course,' I said. 'I'm happy to pay you for your time. Please charge me what you would normally charge someone for an hour of your time.'

She nodded and named a price. As her appearance indicated, she wasn't cheap.

'That's fine. Would you like it now?' I asked, reaching for my bag.

'Yes,' she said simply.

I counted out the money and handed it to her, then I sat back and sipped more wine. It was watery. Probably just as well.

'What proposition?' she asked, after she'd put the money away.

It took me about fifteen minutes to tell her what I wanted. She asked several sensible questions. She was inordinately interested in the fact that I didn't want my husband to touch her.

'Nothing will happen to your marriage if he touches me,' she said. 'Even if he is a handsome millionaire with a huge prick, I will not steal him from you.'

She smiled to show she was making a joke.

'It's not that,' I said. 'It's what would happen to me if I saw him touch you. It would destroy something inside me. One of my links to him. You're young and beautiful and you understand men. I'm older, not beautiful and I've only had limited experience of men. In fact, I've only ever had sex with three men, so I'm not really as… as confident about it as you are.'

'Three men?' she said, thoughtfully. 'Separately or together?'

I don't know why, but I blushed bright red. My face burned hotly.

'Separately,' I said hastily. And then I repeated it. 'Separately.'
She nodded.

'I can promise you this,' she said. 'If you don't want him to touch me, or me to touch him, then he won't and I won't. Okay?'

'Yes, that's fine,' I said.

She opened her bag and took out a diary.

'When is this for?'

I told her and she turned pages. Finally she found the page and looked at me.

'What name?'

I told her. She wrote it down. She wrote some more, then looked at me.

'There are things I need to know.'

'Such as?'

'Will he be clothed or naked? Will he be touching himself? Will he be touching you? Will he masturbate? If so, where will he come?'

'You're very practical,' I said, meaning it. I hadn't thought of some of those things.

She shrugged.

'It's best to know these things before.'

I explained the details to her and I gave her a copy of my husband's list.

She read it quickly, smiling.

'This is a very... male list of lesbian activities. A woman would not make such a list. This is all very visual.'

'Yes, my husband's a very visual person. A lot of what stimulates him is visual.'

'I will do all of these things,' she said matter-of-factly. She then told me to total cost of everything I had asked for. It was a lot of money. She was expensive.

She put the list in the diary page, closed the diary and returned it to her bag. She then sat back and looked up at the ceiling, in thought. She picked up her glass, drained it, then tilted her head back and continued staring at the ceiling.

I refilled her glass, then I topped up my own.

She lowered her gaze and looked at me.

'Have you ever had sex with a woman?'

'No.'

'Have you ever wanted to?'

'I don't know. Is it important?'

'If you want me to pleasure you, yes. If you just want to put on a show for your husband and not have me pleasure you, you will have to fake your pleasure. Can you act?'

'No, not at all. I hadn't thought of that.'

'Well, obviously I can pleasure you to a few orgasms if you want me to. Would your husband want to see that?'

'God, yes. He'd love it.'

'Then I will do that.'

'And what about you? Do you want me to…? To do that for you?'

'That will be up to you. You don't have to do anything for me. You're paying me to give you pleasure and to entertain your husband. I would never tell you what you must do to me or for me. It might be best if you see how you feel on the day. If you want to do something, that will be okay, you can do it and I will like it. If you don't want to do anything, that will also be okay. I won't mind and I will still do what I can to give you pleasure, so your husband can see you enjoying yourself with another woman. I can act very well, so if you want me to pretend, I will do that. Your husband will not know I am acting.'

'I'll take your advice and see how I feel on the day,' I said. 'Which means I have to ask you about… about… how do I say this? About your health.'

She nodded.

'That is good. Some do not ask. What I will do is show you my medical certificate on the day. I go to the clinic once every two months and get a very full check-up. The doctor knows what work I do, so he is very thorough.'

'He knows what you do?'

'Yes. It is best he knows, to do the right tests.'

'Yes, I suppose it is.'

'So don't worry. I will be clean.'

'I'm sure you will,' I said.

'Let me give you my number. Then, if you change your mind, you can let me know.'

'I won't change my mind,' I said. 'Like I said, this is not for me, it's for my husband.'

'I don't think you will change your mind. But things change and it's best to be prepared for change.'

And that was it for the arrangements.

We sat and chatted about nothing in particular for a while. I found out that Kristyna was from Vladivostok and she had no siblings. Her father was dead; a stroke when she was a teenager. Her mother still lived in Vladivostok.

Then we left the room. Kristyna went first, and I waited a few minutes, then I too left. At the reception desk I paid for the room and the unfinished wine, then left the hotel.

Outside, it was late afternoon. For the briefest of moments, the street, the buildings, the air, even the day itself, seemed artificial, like a film set. Then the normality of it asserted itself and my sense of equilibrium returned.

I felt jubilant. I'd done it! I'd arranged something that I thought was impossible to arrange. My husband would be ecstatic.

I wasn't sure how I felt.

Five

Although there's the risk of the age-old accusation, the lady doth protest too much, I'm going to state something quite categorically: I am not a lesbian.

That said, my husband's birthday treat was an absolute success and a delight for everyone concerned. Including me. Especially me.

I'd spent the week before my husband's birthday making all of the necessary arrangements. I booked the bridal suite in a good hotel a few miles from our house. I'd paid for Kristyna's 'services'. My husband hovered about, pretending to help, but what he really wanted was to share the anticipation with me. I wasn't sure I could do that, so I sent him off to his study either to work or to pretend to work – at that moment it didn't matter which.

Then, once the arrangements had been made, I got out a selection of sex toys that I knew my husband liked to watch me using and washed them. Then I charged them. There's nothing worse than a sex toy coming to a halt at the crucial moment. Or any moment, for that matter.

Then I sorted out my clothes, by which I mean underwear, as well as my outer clothes. I had new underwear. Items I would not usually have bought. I put everything I've just mentioned into a small suitcase. Then I put in the other things I'd need for a night away from home, making sure the underwear, which was for my husband's benefit, was on the top.

I keep saying 'my husband'. His name is James. He's a writer. Not a big name, but a name. I was finding it difficult to make eye contact with him. Concerned, he kept asking me if I was all right. I said yes, but I was nervous, excited, apprehensive and, to be totally candid, a little bit scared.

It's not for me, it's not for me, it's not for me, ran through my head like a litany, but it didn't help. Not at all.

The arrangement was that Kristyna would arrive at our hotel room at seven in the evening. I had paid for the room and for her to stay the whole night. She would leave at seven in the morning.

On the actual day itself, we got to the hotel at five in the afternoon and I immediately had a bath and washed my hair. After that, I blow-dried my hair and spent nearly forty-five minutes on my makeup. I applied more than I usually did. I was trying to make myself look a little bit sluttish. When I'd finished, I put on my underwear and stockings. James whistled appreciatively, but after a final look in the well-lit bathroom mirror, I felt the overall effect was more Baby Jane than Baby Doll.

No matter. As I kept telling myself, I wasn't doing it for me.

I carefully put a robe over my slightly-less-than-naked body and waited for Kristyna to arrive.

Six

She certainly knew how to give pleasure.

There were things she did to me that my husband had never done and wouldn't have known how to do, not because he wasn't sensitive to my needs – he was, but because Kristyna was very experienced in pleasure-giving techniques and I responded eagerly to her ministrations. My first orgasm made me whimper. My second made me cry. At one point in the evening, I was face down on the bed with my bottom in the air. Kristyna was kneeling behind me, her tongue probing my roses, and I looked up and saw my husband sitting on a chair at the end of the bed, masturbating furiously, a fevered look in his eyes. I'm not sure he even saw me looking at him. My third orgasm made me scream.

I eventually fell asleep in the early hours of the morning.

When I awoke, Kristyna had gone. James was asleep by my side.

Seven

During the next five years, James, true to his word, never mentioned it once. He didn't allude to it in any way and I was in no hurry to say anything that would give him a pretext to ask me any questions about that night. The only reminder there was of it was in our love-making. James was always rock hard for sex. There had been times before his fifty-fifth birthday when he'd not always been able to achieve a full, firm erection, but since his 'treat' that had not been the case at all. An unforeseen but welcome benefit of me having my orifices licked by a young woman.

I digress.

So, now for a little bit of biography, or what someone once called 'that David Copperfield crap'. As I've already said, my husband, James, is a writer. He's my second husband and we've been married for twenty years.

I had married my first husband, Oliver, when I was nineteen. That I had been too young was something I discovered in my mid-twenties and which was confirmed by the time I was twenty-eight. So I left him. We had a son, Owen. Oliver and I decided we'd be good parents despite being bad spouses. And so, although separated, then divorced, we put on a united front in all parenting matters and as a result, Owen grew up to be a responsible, level-headed young man. Following his father's footsteps, he went into the travel business and sold holidays to people. He was good at it and made a reasonable living. He travelled a lot and was often away from home for two or three weeks at a time. He had a few girlfriends, but no one serious. His job was partly to blame for that, but he enjoyed being single. He was, to use my mother's quaint expression, a confirmed bachelor.

Anyway, the reason I'm mentioning Owen is because he phoned me the day before yesterday and casually mentioned he had a new girlfriend, someone he'd been 'seeing' for a month, someone he really liked. She was a receptionist at a college. He said he wanted to bring her round to our house to meet me and James. I said that'd be very nice, whenever he could arrange it.

'It won't be for a couple of weeks, as I'm off to Tampa for a fortnight,' he said.

'When do you go?' I asked.

'Tomorrow morning. Early'

'Then why don't you come round one weekend once you get back? You can introduce us to your young lady and tell us all about Tampa.'

'I'll do that. You'll like her, mum. She's lovely. Very pretty too. Anyway, I've got to go. Talk soon. Bye.'

And he was gone.

Two minutes later, my phone beeped. It was a message and a photo from Owen. Three words: This is Kristyna.

Because of the spelling, I knew who I was going to see before I opened the photo.

My heart was thumping as I looked at the attached photo.

She was standing with Owen, both of them smiling happily.

It was Kristyna. My Kristyna.

Eight

After I'd managed to regain my composure, I sat and thought about what I should do.

Something or nothing?

The danger with doing nothing was that there was a risk that Owen might find out. That would be very bad – for him and for me. So I had to do something. What I felt I should do was contact Kristyna and tell her she was in a relationship with my son and under no circumstances was he to ever learn that his girlfriend had spent a night in a hotel pleasuring his mother while his mother's husband watched and masturbated. I felt that such a revelation might not be very beneficial to my son's mental well-being. He was level-headed and I wanted him to remain so.

I got up and got my phone. I checked my numbers. No Kristyna. I was puzzled. I knew I hadn't deleted her number, and then I remembered: I'd updated my phone. Kristyna's number was on my old phone. I went to the spare bedroom and opened the bottom drawer. My old phone was in its box with the charger lead. Sometimes, no, always, it pays to be organised and orderly. I took the phone out of the box and switched it on. As I'd expected, it was dead. I plugged it in and started charging it. While it charged I made myself a cup of tea and rehearsed what I was going to say.

It took nearly half an hour to charge to a functioning level, but finally, I was able to locate the number I needed in the contacts list. I copied it into my new phone, then switched off the old phone and returned it to its box and then to its drawer.

I would phone Kristyna tomorrow, once Owen was on his way to Tampa. I'd explain the situation to her. She might decide it was too complicated to stay with Owen because of me. She might refuse to be dishonest with him. She might be willing to pretend she didn't know me. She might…

'Oh, fuck!'

'What is it? It's not like you to swear.'

James was standing in the doorway.

'I was looking for you,' he said, looking around. 'What are you doing in here?'

'Owen's got a new girlfriend. It's Kristyna.'

It took James a split-second.

He looked shocked.

'Oh, fuck.'

'Quite. You're usually more original.'

James ignored that, focusing on the crisis.

'What are you going to do?'

'I'm going to phone her tomorrow and arrange to meet her. Then I'll explain. I'm going to ask her to never mention it to Owen.'

James nodded.

'She might refuse. You know, honesty and all that?'

'I know. And she might want to have nothing more to do with him once she knows I'm his mother. The whole thing might be too complicated for her.'

'It's already too complicated for me,' James said.

'Should I meet her?'

'Of course. You can't stay silent. What happens if he wants to introduce her to his mother?'

'He does, once he gets back from Tampa in a fortnight.'

'When does he go?'

'Tomorrow morning.'

'Is that when you're going to contact her?'

I nodded.

'Good idea? Do you want me to come with you?'

I looked at him.

'Moral support, that's all.' He looked at me steadily. 'No other reason.'

'Thank you, but no. I'll do this on my own. I appreciate you asking though.' I suddenly remembered. 'Why were you looking for me?'

He shrugged.

'It was a grammar question. It doesn't matter now.'

'You might as well try me. I've nothing else to do until tomorrow.'

'Okay. So, is it: An important part of my life has been the people who stood by me, or, An important part of my life have been the people who stood by me?'

'Has,' I was able to say, before I burst into tears. James sat down on the bed next to me and held me tightly. I stayed in his arms for a long time.

Nine

At eight o'clock the next day, I phoned Kristyna. She answered immediately. I identified myself and after a very short pause, during which I imagined she was thinking I was going to request a repeat performance, she asked what I wanted.

'You're in a relationship with my son, Owen.'

She laughed. It was a happy, musical sound.

'We should meet,' she said. 'Are you free later today?'

'Yes,' I said.

'Good. Will you meet me at four?'

'Yes. Where?'

'Can you meet me in the lobby of the hotel where we met?' she asked.

'I'll see you there at four,' I said, ending the call.

Ten

We sat opposite each other the same hotel room. Instead of an ice bucket and a bottle of wine, there was a pot of coffee, milk and sugar on the low table between us.

'I haven't been an escort for over four years,' Kristyna said.

'Was I your last client?' I asked, for some reason feeling quite dejected.

'Almost,' she said cheerfully. 'One or two more, and then I had enough money to go to university.'

'One or two more,' I repeated. 'Separately or together?' I asked.

She smiled.

'Both.'

Her answer flustered me, which served me right.

'Is that what you were doing – saving up for university? Is that why you…?'

'Yes. It paid for my education.'

'That's a high price to pay for an education,' I said.

She shrugged.

'It was not all terrible. Sometimes I had fun. Once or twice I enjoyed myself.'

'I enjoyed myself,' I said. 'Very much.'

'You tasted very nice. I haven't forgotten the taste of you.' As she spoke, her eyes bored into mine.

I stood up. My legs shook.

'Will you do it again?' I asked.

She nodded.

'Yes.'

She did.

Eleven

We left the hotel three hours later. I took her home.

James was the model of discretion. He made no comment, expressed no surprise. He made Kristyna welcome. It was as though the situation was the most natural thing ever. He made us both drinks, then wandered back to his study, leaving us to talk.

We talked a little, with the most important issue, that Owen must never know of our relationship, being agreed upon. Kristyna promised that under no circumstances would she ever let Owen know or suspect the truth.

'He'll introduce us and I'll act as though I have never met you,' she said.

'Are you all right doing that?' I asked.

When she looked at me, her expression was hard.

'No, not really, because I do not want to lie to Owen. But I cannot tell him the truth about us or he will end our relationship. I think we, by which I mean him and me, might have a future together and I don't want to say anything to end that.'

I liked hearing how she spoke about my son and I was pleased that there was the possibility of them having a lasting relationship.

'And I like having fun with you,' she said. 'Which complicates things.'

'Yes, it does.'

'Could I have a bath?' she asked, suddenly very polite, almost shy. 'With you.'

I felt something warm flare up in my chest.

I nodded.

'Yes. I'd like that.' I thought for a moment. 'I need to tell James, so he doesn't walk in and die of shock. I'd like him to get us more drinks – and towels.'

She nodded.

I took her hand and led her to the bathroom.

'I'll find James, tell him, and then I'll join you. Get your clothes off.'

She laughed and started undressing and I had to wrench myself away. I went to James's study and pushed the door open. He was writing. He stopped and looked at me.

He waited.

I decided to make light of it.

'We're going to have a bath. Could you make us more drinks and get us two of the really big bath towels, please?'

James grinned hugely.

'Two drinks and two towels coming right up,' he said.

'You still can't touch her,' I said. 'Not ever.'

James shook his head.

'I wasn't going to,' he said, and again I could see he meant it.

'Hold me,' I said and slipped into his arms.

'Are you going to be all right?' he whispered.

I looked up at him.

'I don't know,' I said. 'I have no idea what I'm doing. All I know is that it makes me feel good, so I want it while I can have it. I can have it, can't I?'

James nodded.

'Yes, but I want you to be careful. I don't want this to hurt you.'

'I'll try and be careful,' I said. 'Although I think it's a bit late for that.'

'Yeah, well, you know what they say?'

'No. What do they say?'

'Character determines destiny.'

I thought about that for a minute.

'Which 'they' said that?'

'Heraclitus. Allegedly.'

'Clever man. Now, drinks and towels. It's bath time for the bitches.'

And I was out of the study and on my way to the bathroom, pulling my clothes off as I ran.

Twelve

By the time James came into the bathroom with our drinks and our towels, Kristyna and I were sitting in the bath. I was resting my back against the bath and Kristyna was leaning back against me. I was gently stroking her breasts.

'Drinks. Towels.'

'Thank you kind sir,' I said, as James put the glasses in our hands. He turned and hung the towels on the hooks on the back of the door. He pulled the door open to leave when Kristyna spoke, halting him in his tracks.

'If you'd like to stay just a bit longer,' she said, standing up. 'I was just about to give your wife a good soaping. You can stay and watch if you like.'

'I like,' James said, closing the door.

I stood up and handed Kristyna the soap.

'Bend over,' she said. 'We start from the bottom and work our way up.'

Grinning at James, I bent over.

Thirteen

James fell asleep before us.

It was five minutes past three in the morning when I cuddled up to him, with Kristyna behind me, her arm around my waist.

I thought of the stupidity of what we were doing, of the sheer pleasure of what we were doing, of the purity of it, of the honesty of it, and of the dishonesty of it. I loved what she did to me and what she did for me and I liked what I did for her. James obviously loved it too. He looked like a man who couldn't believe his luck. Every night he watched his wife and a very lovely-looking young woman make love. He was on the bed with us, so close he could have reached out hand touched us, but he never did. I could see he wanted to, but he knew, as did I, that if he ever did, it would be over. Kristyna would leave and our lesbian fantasy interlude would evaporate, leaving nothing but a bitter residue.

Fourteen

Every evening, once she had spoken to Owen on the phone, Kristyna would come round to our house and stay the night. We'd have a bath and go to bed. James would watch us pleasure each other.

That was the situation for the two weeks that Owen was in Florida.

As I was drying myself, I asked Kristyna what she intended to do once he got back from Tampa.

'I will stop coming here and go and see your son instead.'

I felt a twinge of jealousy when she said that. Then I felt ashamed that I felt jealous of my own son.

Once we were in bed together and Kristyna started doing what she did so well, I forgot about everything else and simply enjoyed the pleasures she gave me.

And then Owen came back.

Fifteen

The first change was the one Kristyna had said would happen: she stopped coming around in the evenings. She went to Owen's instead. That's what people in new – and old – relationships do – they spend time together. No matter – to me it felt like a betrayal, even though I was the real betrayer in this sorry saga.

The second change was the one in James. He wanted to make love all the time. My times with Kristyna had an aphrodisiac effect on him. He was constantly erect. We no longer made love – we fucked – hard, rough coupling that felt really good and was very satisfying.

The third change was in me. I knew I was falling for Kristyna in a big way. I thought about her most of the time. I replayed scenes from our moments together, eating, drinking, bathing, drying each other, kissing, as well as our much more intimate moments.

It made the moment that Owen introduced her to us potentially awkward, but somehow we managed to handle it with enough naturalness to make it seem a very natural encounter.

I could see that Owen adored Kristyna and it seemed that she thought a lot of him, but obviously, with her, it was hard to judge her real feelings for my son.

Anyway, our introduction went well and I could that my son was relieved that I had tacitly given his new girlfriend my seal of approval.

They stayed for a couple of hours, and they both seemed happy when they left.

Sixteen

The next development occurred when Owen had to go to France for fourteen days. He had to go to Poitiers and inspect an apartment, to make sure its refurbishment was completed in time for a holiday-maker to move into for a month.

He left on a Thursday evening, and that night, Kristyna was back in our bed, making me feel wonderful. James sat at the foot of the bed and watched our libido-driven contortions.

Those fourteen days that Owen was away in Poitiers were absolutely beautiful. Perfect.

Seventeen

That was the pattern of my life for the next year. Kristyna went to work, then went to Owen's and stayed with him. When he was away, she came to ours and took me to bed. And Owen never knew. Never suspected.

And things would have continued like that indefinitely. But, like all truly wonderful things and like all truly terrible things, it came to an abrupt end. And again, there's no one to blame, not really. I could apportion blame, I suppose, but I'd have had to start by blaming myself, and that was something I was not prepared to do.

Kristyna was in bed with me when she casually mentioned that Owen was taking her on holiday for a week.

'When?' I asked, trying to sound unconcerned, but not doing a very good job of it.

'Next week. On Saturday.'

'Where are you going?'

'To a small town in the south of France.'

'I hope you have a wonderful time,' I said.

'Thank you. I think I will.'

And so the first discordant note was sounded.

Eighteen

While they went off on holiday and stayed in a luxurious hotel in the small town in the south of France for a week, and while Owen was going all out to impress his not-so-new girlfriend, I counted the days they were away.

'You need to end it,' James said. 'You need to finish your relationship with her.'

We were having breakfast on the second day they were away. James had just listened to me extolling Kristyna's virtues and he'd patiently heard me saying that she'd be home in five days and he'd put his coffee cup down, looked at me very steadily and said those words.

'How can you say that? You know what she means to me.'

James nodded.

'Yes, I do.' He paused. 'That's why I'm saying it. You're in a very dangerous situation. Nothing good can come from it.'

'It is good,' I said. 'It makes me feel good. Surely that counts for something?'

'Yes, it does. But you're ignoring the reality in order to enjoy the fantasy. Do you honestly believe your relationship with Kristyna can continue indefinitely without Owen finding out?'

'Yes,' I said fervently. 'It has continued and he hasn't found out. So yes, I do think that.'

'You're fucking your son's girlfriend,' James said. It was a brutal sentence and the way he said it made it lie there in the morning light in all its ugliness.

'There's no need to say it like that,' I said, defensively.

'There's every need to say it as it is,' James said, 'because you're pretending it's something else.'

'I'm in a romance that is very good for me.'

'You're fucking your son's girlfriend. You're cheating on your own son, making him a cuckold and you're encouraging his girlfriend to cheat on him and lie to him.'

'And you're a hypocrite. I see how excited you get. You can't hide your huge erections. What we do excites you and you enjoy it.'

'Yes, that's true. You're right. What you and Kristyna do together turns me on. I love watching you together. When you sat on her face and screamed as you orgasmed last night, I was harder than I've ever been. It was beautiful. When your naked bodies are entwined and you're pleasuring each other, I think I'm in some sort of pleasure heaven – but that doesn't mean that I don't realise how dangerous it is for you, and Owen, and Kristyna. I don't want it to end either. I love it. What man wouldn't? But potentially it could destroy all three of you – and any chance you will ever have of having relationships based on trust and respect and love.'

'I trust and respect and love them both.'

'You don't respect your son, or you wouldn't treat him so badly.'

'He doesn't know!'

'Just because someone doesn't realise they're being abused doesn't mean they're not being abused. The not knowing is the key to abusers being able to continue abusing.'

'I am *not* abusing my son.'

'Then let's give him the facts and ask his opinion, shall we?'

'Why are you doing this?'

'I should have done it a long time ago.'

'I love her.'

'I know. It won't be easy, but you've got to do it. For Owen's sake.'

'I don't know if I can.'

'You can. And you will.'
'Oh! And you're going to force me to give her up, are you?'
'Yes,' James said softly. 'If I have to.'
'What?'
'You heard me.'

I didn't answer. So it had finally come to a point where I had to make a choice; my husband or my lover. My son's well-being or my sexual gratification. Choices. Choices.

Finally, I looked up at James.

'You know I'm right,' he said softly.

I nodded.

'I'll tell her when they get back.'

Nineteen

Once again, we sat opposite each other in the leather wing chairs in the same hotel room. Once again, there was a pot of coffee, milk and sugar on the low table between us.

I sat upright, trying to convey authority. Kristyna was sitting quite primly. She was wearing a brown suit. She looked like an accountant. She took a diary out of her bag and placed it on the table next to her cup, then waited.

'I want to end our relationship,' I said.

'Do you?'

'No, not really, but I think it would be best if we had a proper relationship, rather than the one we've got – or rather, the one we had.'

'A proper relationship?'

'Yes, Proper. The kind of relationship that a woman usually has with her son's girlfriend.'

'And what does that involve?'

'I don't know, but I'm pretty sure it doesn't involve you ramming a huge dildo into my vagina and saying, 'Lick my pussy, bitch.'

Kristyna smiled.

'Yes, I liked that evening very much too. I had five orgasms. A personal record.'

I felt I was losing control of the conversation.

'We need to end it,' I said firmly. 'For Owen's sake.'

'I see. You're worried about your son?'

'Yes. Well, I'm worried about him finding out. It'll destroy him.'

'Owen and I have a very good relationship. He says that the way we make love is like nothing he's ever known. He's very conventional. He would just have sex in the missionary position all the time. I do with him everything I do with you. He is getting a good sex education.'

'Why are you telling me that?'

'Because you said you were worried about your son. I want you to know he is very happy, very content, very in love, very well looked after, very well cared for, very loved.'

'You make him sound like an invalid.'

'I am helping him leave his invalid state and become a whole person. As I helped you leave yours.'

'Yes, you did. I know exactly what you've done for me, but we need to… to adjust our relationship. I want it to be 'conventional'. I want to meet you for lunch or occasionally. I'd like to go shopping with you now and again, or a walk. That sort of thing.'

'No more sex?'

'No, no more sex.'

'A platonic relationship? Friends?'

'More than friends, I hope. We have a connection that's based on more than carnal gratification.'

'No.'

'No what?'

'No, you can't end it.'

'What are you talking about? We can't go on as we are. Surely you understand that?'

'No, I do not.'

'You must.'

I stood up.

'Please sit back down,' Kristyna said icily. 'You're not fully understanding the situation. Let me explain.'

'There's nothing to explain,' I said angrily. 'I'm going. It's over. Get used to it.'

Kristyna held up her phone.

'Sit down now, or I'll call your son and tell him that you and I have been having a lesbian sexual relationship for many years, long before I met him, and that you refused to end it and forced me to hide this fact from him.'

I sat back down.

'You don't need to do that,' I said. 'What do you want?'

Kristyna nodded in satisfaction.

'There's a lot to explain,' she said. 'But let's be very clear about one thing; it's not over, not until I say it is, so get used to it.'

'Why are you doing this?'

'I like our relationship. I don't want it to end. I like having sex with you and I like having sex with your son. I've trained you both well. I have no wish for anything to change.'

I stood up.

'Right. So it continues? It's a mistake, but okay. I've clearly got no choice.'

'I asked you to sit down. You're not leaving yet.'

'What?' I asked, disbelieving.

Kristyna opened the diary that was on the table and took out a piece of paper.

'My bank details. I need you to make a bank transfer now.' She named a large sum of money.

'Blackmail?'

She nodded.

'Money and sex. The two staples in life. In exchange, I will continue to make sure that your son neither suspects nor finds out about us.'

'Is that it?'

'For now. I'm sure I'll think of other things. When I do, I'll let you know what they are.'

She paused and sipped her coffee.

'Just to be totally clear,' she said. 'I expect absolute obedience from you. If I tell you to do something, I expect you to do it immediately. No hesitation. If you ever disobey me, I will phone your son, tell him about our relationship and I'll say that you forced me to hide it from him, even though I wanted to be totally honest with him. Then I'll say the whole thing is too complex for me – and that I can't possibly stay in a relationship with him because of his perverted mother. And then I'll simply up and go, out of his life forever. Neither of you will ever hear from me again. You can then explain everything to your devastated son. Good luck trying to put those broken pieces back together.'

'You're vile,' I said, shocked.

'And you're my bitch, so get undressed.'

'What?'

'You heard me. Get undressed and get on the bed. I feel like having my pussy licked and you do it so well. Not as well as your son, but well enough.'

Feeling nothing but disgust at my own weakness, I slowly got undressed.

Twenty

'Call her bluff,' James said when I told him.

'I would, but it's too risky. It might not be a bluff. Then what?'

'So you're going to pay her for the dubious privilege of being her sex slave?'

'Yes, if it means Owen doesn't find out.'

'Let him find out. Use her own threat against her. Tell him that she coerced you to have a lesbian relationship with her, and that she extorted money from you. I'll back you up. In fact, call the police. Let them deal with her.'

'I've no proof of what I've said. She was careful to leave no evidence.'

'You just paid a large sum of money into her bank account. That's evidence of coercion or blackmail.'

'She's my son's girlfriend and they're talking about setting up home together. A potential mother-in-law putting money into her future daughter-in-law's bank account is no proof of anything. It's probably quite commonplace.'

'So you're simply going to go along with what she wants?'

'I don't see that I have a choice.'

'Stop her in her tracks. Tell her to fuck off. Tell her to go ahead and tell Owen. I don't think she will.'

'Why not?'

'Because she's using him, just as she's using you.'

'For sex and money?'

'I don't know. But she's managed to get a pretty good life established with him. When you met her she was an escort. Now look at where she is and what she's got. She got a university education which you said she paid for with money for sex. She's got a good job as a college receptionist, she's got a man and a woman on a rota servicing her sexually, and now she's found a way to force you give her financial support. What's next?'

'I don't know.'

'Based on what she's done so far, I think she'll move in with Owen and make his life a sheer delight, while keeping you as her sexual and financial slave. Then after a while, maybe a year, maybe not as long as that, she'll suggest they get married and he'll agree to it. And then she'll either stay with him, or she'll clean him out and clear off.'

'A rather bleak view.'

'A rather realistic view,' James said. 'And I don't think her demand for money from you will be her last. There'll be more. And the amounts that she'll want will increase.'

Twenty One

The same hotel room again.

'I want you to transfer some more money into my account.'

'How much?' I asked dully.

'Double what you put in last time.'

'No.'

Kristyna said nothing. She simply picked up her phone and searched her contacts. Then she pressed a button.

'All right,' I said, defeated. 'I'll pay it.'

Kristyna switched her phone off.

'How long are you going to keep demanding money from me?'

'For as long as I like,' she said curtly. 'I told you: I'll give you an order and you'll follow it instantly. Failure to obey will result in me punishing you, ruining your life, destroying your family.'

'You're already ruining my life and destroying my family. Why? What did I ever do to you?'

'Why am I doing it? Because you made it possible. You let me.'

'No, I mean *why* are *you* doing it? What's driving you?'

'Why do I want money and sex? That's a strange question. Those are the things life has to offer that I like very much. I don't really care about anything else, but those two things do interest me greatly.'

'But there are other ways to get them with exploiting someone – without exploiting me.'

Kristyna nodded.

'Yes, there are. I know that very well. I worked as an 'escort' for five years. That's how long it took me to save enough money to pay for my three years of university education. And that was at a university with the lowest fees. And I had to continue to work as an escort while I studied for my degree. Several students I knew paid to fuck me, some of them on a regular basis. One student fucked me in all my holes one night and then discussed feminism and women's rights in a seminar the next day. So I know there are ways to 'earn' money, but it's easier to find a way to get someone to simply give it to you.'

'Do you actually love my son? Do you have any feelings for him at all, or are you using him too?'

'That's none of your business.'

'My son is none of my business!'

'My feelings about anything, including your son, are none of your business. Anyway, enough of this. Pay me my money now. Transfer it into my account, then get undressed and lay down on the bed.'

I used my phone to transfer the money, and then I took my clothes off. I went to the bed.

'Face down, whore!'

I lay face down.

Kristyna stood by the side of the bed, then reached beneath it. She pulled out a cane.

'I did not like you refusing me just now, so now I intend to punish you. I am going to cane you hard. After each stroke you will say thank you, and then you will ask for another. You will say: 'Thank you. Another.' Understand?'

I nodded.

'Tell me you understand.'

'I understand.'

She rested the cane on my buttocks. The wood felt cold on my skin. She raised the cane and brought it down hard on my bottom. It stung, burned. I yelped.

'Say it!'

I gasped for breath. The pain was hot and intense, like a line of fire.

'Thank you. Another.'

Another hard, hot stroke. I could feel my right buttock flaming red. Tears welled in my eyes.

'Thank you. Another.'

She stopped after twelve strokes, and I'm certain it was because her arm was tired, not because of my tears.

Twenty Two

She went out of her way to humiliate me that day, starting with making me pay the money into her account, followed by her caning me and making me thank her for each cane stroke and to then beg for another. I endured it all, but I felt she had broken something inside me; as though she caned a piece of my personality, my identity, into non-existence.

And then, if that wasn't enough, it seemed she felt the 'punishment' she had meted out hadn't fully taught me a lesson. So she made sure I totally degraded myself before she allowed me to leave that room.

Once she had finished caning me, she had said I could get dressed and leave, but only if I crawled off the bed and crossed the room on my hands and knees.

I did as she said, acutely aware of my burning bottom sticking up in the air as I inelegantly crawled on my hands and knees across the room to the chair that had my clothes piled on it. I tried my hardest to hold in my tears and sobs as I dressed, but I was only partly successful.

Once I was dressed, she continued with my humiliation. She inspected me and shook her head sadly.

'Very disappointing,' she said. 'I think,' she added, as though it was an afterthought, but I could tell from the glint in her eyes that it had been carefully planned, 'I think you're too old for me. Your wrinkles and your lines are really quite noticeable in daylight. And your body is quite old and saggy, isn't it? I noticed it when I was caning you. Should I look for someone younger, do you think? Someone with smooth skin and supple flesh?'

I stayed silent. The anger I felt at her comments was like a white-hot rage inside me. I wanted to slap her hard or punch her in the face. I stared at her and I had the satisfaction of seeing her take an involuntary step back. A fleeting look of uncertainty crossed her face. And then it was gone and her arrogant, cruel personality reasserted itself.

'Right, I have things to do,' she said brusquely. 'Fuck off, whore.'

I said nothing. I simply left the room.

There had to be a way.

Twenty Three

Owen and Kristyna went on another holiday. This time it was to Croatia. Another luxury hotel, this time for two weeks.

I imagined Kristyna's behind-the-scenes machinations; the web of deceit and the dissembling she had deployed to persuade Owen to take her away again at his considerable expense, and I longed to find a way to stop her in her tracks.

I did not want her in my son's life. She was fleecing him. She was doing to him psychologically what she had done to me physically and emotionally.

My cane welts still stung. They hurt when I walked.

James was furious. He wanted to call the police.

'This abuse has to stop!' he said, as he bathed my welts and put antiseptic cream on them.

'That will make it worse. If the police get involved, everything will come out. My son will never forgive me. How could he?'

My phone rang.

I froze.

'I'll get it,' James said, an aggressive edge to his voice.

'If it's her, don't say anything. Owen will hear.'

I quickly threw on a bathrobe.

James picked my phone up and thumbed the button.

'Hi James,' I heard Owen say. 'Is mum there?'

'Hi Owen. Yes, I'll hand you over.'

James passed me the phone.

'So how's the holiday?' I asked.

'It's great,' Owen said. 'Have you ever seen a wolf?'

'A wolf? No.'

'Great. Well, I've just seen a wolf and I thought I'd just call you and let you see it.'

'There's a wolf near you?'

'Yes, they have them here. Lynxes too, but I haven't seen any of those yet.'

'Please be careful.'

'It's okay. They've got rangers here. They don't attack humans. The wolves, I mean.' He laughed. 'Anyway, there's a wolf in one of the clearings. Do you want to see it?'

'I suppose so,' I said. 'Where's your young lady?'

'She was a bit nervous, so she stayed at the café. I'm going back there in a minute, once you've seen it.'

My phone screen went blurry for a split-second, and then it was filled with greens and browns. Then my son, looking relaxed and cheerful was looking at me. He was surrounded by what looked like a forest.

'Hi mum. So, are you ready to see your first real live wolf?'

'Yes, I suppose so. As long as it's not too close?'

'They can't jump through phones.'

'I wasn't thinking of me,' I said quietly.

The phone tilted and I was looking at a mass of tree trunks and foliage. There was a clearing. At first, I didn't see it because of its colouring. And then I did.

It was huge. It was standing with its front paws on a boulder and was glaring at Owen. The distance was too great to see its eyes clearly, but I could see that they were yellow and that they stayed fixed unwaveringly on Owen. Drool hung in runners from its muzzle and its pale tongue lolled out of one side.

'Can you see it?' Owen asked, excitedly. 'Look at it; it's awesome.'

I could hear the child he had been in his voice and I felt a surge of maternal love and fear for him go through me and I wanted nothing more at that moment but to somehow transport myself there and stand between him and any danger.

'Yes, I can see it,' I said, needing to say something normal, something that didn't give away my feelings.

'Are you okay, mum?' Owen asked, ever perceptive. 'You sound weird.'

'I'm just a little nervous for you,' I said. 'Could you start making your way to the café now?' I asked.

The camera lurched and turned and I was looking at my son again.

'Right, I've got to go. I just wanted to show you a real live wolf.'

'Thank you,' I said. 'And now have a good holiday.'

'Will do. Bye mum. Love you. Bye James. Don't love you.'

And he was gone.

Twenty Four

There were a couple more phone calls during the holiday. It was only during the last one that Kristyna came into view and said hello. I said hello back and said that I hoped she was having a lovely holiday. She said she was, thanks to my wonderful son. And then she was gone.

Owen and I conversed for a bit longer and then he ended the call.

Two more days and they were back.

Twenty Five

The wedding announcement wasn't a surprise.
I'd been dreading it, but expecting it.
Owen and Kristyna came round to tell us.
James and I were suitably happy and celebratory. There wasn't a false note from either of us. We opened a bottle of champagne and celebrated the wonderful news. We toasted the happy couple and wished them a long and happy life together.
I told Kristyna she was very lucky, and she agreed.
'He's wonderful,' she said. 'And he's wonderful to me.'
James told Owen he was a lucky man and he agreed.
'She's lovely,' he said. 'Very lovely.'
They stayed for an hour and it was an absolutely delightful evening.

Twenty Six

It was two days later that James came out of his study and said:

'Come with me.'

I could tell from his tone that it was important, so I got up quickly and followed him into his study. He indicated I should sit down on his office chair.

I sat down and looked at his computer screen. It took me a few moments to work out what I was seeing.

It was an escort agency's profile page of one of their 'models'. The agency's name was *Silk Butterflies*. The profile was Kristyna's profile. There were twelve photos, five of which were quite... revealing.

'Have a good read through,' James said. 'You may need a sick-bag.'

I sat there and read the page in its entirety.

Twenty Seven

Silk Butterflies Model Profile: Kristyna

Hello, my name is Kristyna, I am an independent Russian model. I am a very cheerful and happy young woman. I will enjoy making all of your wildest fantasies come true. I provide a very discreet, exclusive and tasteful service. My photos are 100% real and are updated monthly. I would be your ideal companion for a very enjoyable and intense experience. Feel free to contact me on the number next to my profile photo. I am looking forward to meeting you. Love and kisses, Kristyna.

About Kristyna:

> Gender: Female
> Sexual Orientation: Bisexual
> Age:28
> Hometown: Vladivostok
> Eyes: Brown
> Hair: Blonde
> Breasts: Size B, Natural breasts
> Pubic hair: Shaved completely
> Language: English
> Ethnicity: European (white)
> Nationality: Russian
> Height: 177 cm / 5'8"
> Weight: 55 kg (121.25 lb)
> Smoking: Non-smoker
> Drinking: Sometimes
> Tattoos: No
> Piercings: No

Availability:

    Available for men (individual or group)
    Couples (man and woman)

Locations:

    Hotel
    Home Visits

Kristyna's services:

    Oral sex
    Come in mouth
    Come on face
    Come on body
    Swallow
    Deep French kissing
    Anal sex
    Licking anus
    69 sex position
    Striptease/Lapdance
    Erotic massage
    Golden shower
    Threesome/foursome/group
    Foot fetish
    Sex toys
    Domination

Rates:

1 hour: 300
1.5 hours: 500
2 hours: 700
Overnight: 1500

Kristyna's Latest Reviews (updated 2 days ago):

Wonderful. Lovely young woman. Made me feel fantastic. 5 stars, no question. (Sept 12th)

Amazing 5 star experience! Kristyna is very elegant and has a great energy. Head and shoulders above most women. (Sept 14th)

A great stag-do party girl. We all loved Kristyna and would book her again for a party. Lots of enthusiasm and energy. 5 stars without question. (Sept 20th)

Delicious young lady, all natural, no tattoos, super clean, slim and beautiful. Really nice young woman who I couldn't keep my hands off. Full marks, full stars. (Oct 2nd)

Kristyna made me and my wife very relaxed and happy. A perfect companion, delightful company. No hesitation in giving 5 stars. (Oct 7th)

Kristyna is happy to do a lot of thing most women won't do. She's truly amazing. 5 stars, but only because I can't give her 10. (Oct 9th)

Twenty Eight

I looked at James.

'This is really awful, but it's also exactly what I need. Thank you for finding it.'

'You ain't seen nothin' yet,' James said. 'But I have to warn you: you're not going to like it.'

I braced myself.

'Go on, I need to know. What is it?'

'Look at the dates.'

I looked at the dates, but didn't understand.

I looked at James.

'When did Owen go to Tampa?' James asked gently.

The penny dropped and I scrutinised the review dates. Every one of them was a date on which Owen had been out of the country.

'So, it begs the question: does she really work in a college as a receptionist? And if so, which college?'

I realised I didn't know.

'I don't know.'

'My guess is she doesn't. Based on this, I'd say that she's never given up being an escort.'

I remembered the sex Kristyna and I had had and I shuddered. I suddenly felt sick as the words to one of the reviews sounded in my mind in a deep male voice.

A great stag-do party girl. We all loved Kristyna and would book her again for a party. Lots of enthusiasm and energy.

Fighting back tears, I looked at James.

'She's a prostitute. And she's still working as one. I can't let my son marry a prostitute.'

James stayed silent.

'Is there a way that this can be sent anonymously to my son?'

'There might be,' James said finally, 'but that's a very dangerous path to go down. Why don't you just send it to him yourself and say someone anonymous sent it to you?'

'Because he'd hate me for doing that. He'd never stop blaming me for destroying his dream.'

'But you'll have saved him from a life of misery. From ruin. Humiliation.'

'He won't see it like that.'

'He might.'

'He won't. James! I know he won't. I don't know what to do. I think it would be best if he got it anonymously. That way I can never be blamed and it'll mean that if he needs to talk to me about it, he'll be able to as the actual revelation won't have come from me and will have nothing to do with me.'

James pondered for a while.

'In that case, I'll ask Edward how to send an anonymous email.'

Edward was James's IT technician.

'Thank you.'

Twenty Nine

'I've sent it anonymously,' James told me the following evening. 'It can't be traced back to me.'

'Are you sure?'

'Positive. Edward reassured me on that.'

'Did he ask why you needed to know how to do that?'

'No. He's far too discrete.'

'Let's see what happens now, shall we?'

'Be prepared for nothing to happen,' James said. 'And be prepared for everything to happen.'

'I'll try,' I said.

Thirty

I heard nothing for over a week and then Owen phoned.

He told me he was going to Paris for a week, then Prague the following week.

'One after the other?' I asked.

'In Paris for six days, back home for one day, then off to Prague for seven days.'

There was a note of impatience in his voice.

'Are you all right? You sound a bit impatient or irritated, I'm not sure which.'

'No, I'm fine. No, I am a bit annoyed actually.'

My heart thudded.

'Why?'

'Well, it's nothing really. One of my friends pranked me. Not sure who.'

'Oh? What was the prank?'

'It was a stupid one. Whoever it was sent me a link to a fake profile page on an Escort Agency website. They'd put Kristyna on there. As though she was one of the escorts.'

'Oh, that's a mean trick,' I said.

'Well, yeah, but a prank's a prank, you know. It's quite funny, I suppose, but I can't work out who sent it. It was an anonymous email. And no one's admitting they did it. I don't mind them sending it, but I'd just like to know who it was.'

'Is Kristyna all right? She wasn't too offended, was she?'

'Nah. She's okay. Once I explained that it was one of my friends who was maybe a bit jealous, probably one who fancies her himself, she was fine. I said you wait till you see what they say at the wedding. I had to explain the best man tradition of disparaging the groom – sometimes at the bride's expense.'

'It's not long now, is it? How do you feel?'

'Yeah, actually okay. I really love her, mum. She's brilliant. And she really likes you too.'

'And I really like her,' I lied.

I was amazed at how easily that lie came, but I was glad that it did. It sounded authentic.

'Neither of us is religious, but we're having a short – a very short – church service in that church near mine. Holy Cross, I think it's called, or something like that. It's two streets away. It's Russian Orthodox, and they do an Anglican wedding service, whatever that is. Anyway, the main point is that it's a short service. Very short. Thirty minutes tops.'

'And is that what you both want?'

'To be honest, Kristyna's not that bothered either, but she says her mother will expect to see her having a traditional wedding, so that's the real reason we're doing it.'

'Will her mother be there?'

'No. Her mother's in Vladivostok and can't travel. She's going to watch it on a video link. The church will set it up. Video cameras, sound. It's all arranged. They're recording it for us too.'

'It all sounds very lovely.'

'It will be. I take it your invitation hasn't arrived yet?'

'No, not yet.'

'You'll probably get it tomorrow then.'

'I'm looking forward to it.'

Thirty One

You are cordially invited

to the wedding of

Owen
Hadley-Stratton

and

Kristyna
Arkadyevna Kochesok

on 15th May

at 1pm

at The Church of the Holy Cross
Tower Street

Reception to follow

Thirty Two

'Cock a sock!' James snorted. 'Ha! No wonder she kept that quiet. And no wonder she wants to change it. Kristyna Cock-a-Sock. Seems appropriate.'

He burst out laughing again and then saw my expression.

'Look, I'm sorry, but I really don't think there's anything more we can do. They're going to get married and all we can hope is that with Owen she's genuine, that she really loves him and that she'll stay with him and make him happy.'

'What about what she does when he's away?' I asked.

'We don't know for sure. For all we know, they could all be fake reviews. But that's not the point.'

'What is? The fact we can't do anything?'

'Yes.'

I was close to considering that he might be right, but I wasn't ready to admit anything just yet, not to James and most definitely not to myself.

'Has she demanded money recently?'

'Not for nearly a month.'

'She may not ask for any more. Once they're married, she might find it quite difficult to explain how money from you got into her account.'

I wasn't convinced, but I let it pass without comment.

The problem I had was I'd seen her vile side, her evil side and I knew she was wrong for Owen. I wasn't the only woman who'd deceived my son; she had also deceived him in so many different ways. Their marriage would be built on lies and deceit. I wanted my son to have a marriage based on love and trust. He didn't have that and he'd never have that with Kristyna Cock-a-Sock.

'Come on,' James said. 'They're going to get married and you can't stop them. If you try, they'll just become even more determined. You risk driving them closer.'

I stared at nothing.

'I can't do nothing,' I said. 'But I feel so helpless because I don't know what to do.'

'That's because there is nothing you can do. You've done what you can and nothing's changed. They're getting married. Unless you directly and categorically tell your son everything about her, he'll marry her. Are you going to tell him?'

'No. I can't. It'll destroy our relationship.'

'In that case, you're the mother of the groom. What you need to do now is think about what you're going to wear to the wedding? Which dress? Which shoes? You have to look better than everyone else except the bride, which shouldn't be too difficult for you.'

'Sometimes you're a real bastard and at other times you're incredibly sweet,' I said. 'And sometimes, like now, you can be both at the same time.'

'Yep,' James said happily.

I spent the rest of the evening deciding which dress I was going to wear.

Thirty Three

I held James's hand as the vicar said the relevant words to Owen and Kristyna.

She was radiantly beautiful in her pearl white dress and Owen was very handsome in his charcoal suit. They definitely looked good together. Very good.

Owen's best friend, Daniel, was the best man and he stood slightly behind them and slightly to one side. I was pleased Owen had chosen Daniel because Daniel was one of Owen's more sensible and reliable friends. I knew his reception speech would not be too disparaging of either Owen or Kristyna, and oddly, I was relieved.

Perhaps a wedding does that, gives those not getting married a degree of hope that things in life are not all bad; that there is much that is good and much to be celebrated.

As I watched the best man take the ring out of the small box he was holding and pass it to Owen, I idly wondered if I was the only mother-in-law who'd had a screaming orgasm as she'd sat naked astride her daughter-in-law's face. I wasn't conceited enough to actually think I was the only one in the entire world, but I thought it was very likely that I was in a very, very exclusive club – a club I wholeheartedly wished I did not belong to. But character determines destiny, so I did belong to it.

'I will now refer to the marriage liturgy from *The Book of Common Prayer*,' the vicar announced, 'when I say before God and in all sincerity, should anyone present know of any reason that this couple should not be joined in Holy matrimony, speak now or forever hold your peace.'

I stood up.

James tried to pull me back down, but I yanked my hand free.

'I know of a reason,' I said loudly. 'In fact I know lots of reasons.'

There were shocked murmurs and mutterings from the gathered fifty or so people. Owen turned and glared at me, rightly but wrongly furious, his fists clenched so hard his knuckles were white. I stared at Kristyna and she tried to hold my gaze, but she couldn't. She had counted on my being submissive, obedient, cowed by the force of her personality and by her insidious hold over me – admittedly a hold over me that I had allowed her to have. But she was nothing but a money-grabbing, blackmailing whore, one that strangers fucked regularly when my son was away from home. I'd had the misfortune of reading her reviews.

Kristyna will do a lot of thing most women won't do. She's amazing. 5 stars, but only because I can't give her 10.

No mother wants her son to marry a whore.

'Then please speak,' the vicar said, trying not to show how shaken and upset he was by what he clearly regarded as a breach of protocol, despite it being his church's tradition. 'If you truly believe that this couple should not be joined in Holy matrimony, please go ahead and state your reason.'

There was absolute silence.

'There's neither blame nor guilt on anyone's part for what happened,' I said. 'And even if I were to want to apportion blame, I can't think who the right person to blame would be. But I don't want to point any accusing fingers because at the time everyone had a very lovely time, especially James, my husband. Kristyna, the bride, also enjoyed herself immensely…'

R J Dent is a poet, novelist, translator, essayist, and short story writer. As a renowned translator of European literature, he has published modern English translations of *The Songs of Maldoror* (Le Comte de Lautréamont); *Speculations* (Alfred Jarry); *Capital of Pain* (Paul Éluard); *Her Three Daughters* (Pierre Louÿs); *Soluble Fish* (André Breton); *The Dead Man* (Georges Bataille); *Stories, Tales and Fables* (Marquis de Sade); *The Monk* (Antonin Artaud); *Poems & Fragments* (Alcaeus); *Selected Erotic Poems* (Charles Baudelaire); and major works by Louis Aragon, Maurice Rollinat and Tarjei Vesaas.

As a poet and novelist, R J Dent is the author of a poetry collection, *Moonstone Silhouettes*; a novel, *Myth*; a short collection, *Gothiques and Fantastiques*; and *Screaming at the Window*, a true crime book about Blanche Monnier: the Prisoner of Poitiers.

R J Dent's official website is; www.rjdent.com

An Excerpt From Andre Breton's 'Soluble Fish',
Translated by R J Dent and available from Incunabula

20

One day a young man made the effort to collect the downy fuzz of certain fruits in a white earthenware bowl. He then rubbed the fruit fuzz on several mirrors, until they were coated with a sort of mist. Then he went off and when he returned quite a long time later, the mirrors had disappeared.

The mirrors had got up one after the other and had left, trembling. Much later, another young man admitted that, on returning from work, he had found one of those mirrors which had approached imperceptibly. He had then picked it up and taken it to his home.

He was a young apprentice who was very handsome in his red overalls which made him look like a basin full of water that a wound had been cleaned in. The surface of the water had swirled like a thousand birds in a tree with submerged roots. He had managed to get the mirror up the flights of stairs where he lived, although he did remember that two doors, each with a thin glass plate around the handle, had slammed as he had passed them on his way up to the single room he occupied on the seventh floor.

He had had to stretch both arms wide apart in order to carry his load, which he placed with the utmost care in a corner of the room, after which he went to bed.

He didn't close his eyes all night long.

The mirror reflected itself to an unfathomable depth and an incredible distance. The cities had only time enough to make their appearance between two of its layers: fever cities traversed in every directions by solitary women; abandoned cities; cities of genius too, the buildings of which were surmounted by animated statues and had freight elevators which had been designed to resemble human beings; cities of appalling storms; and one city more beautiful and more fleeting than any of the others, full of palaces and with all of its factories shaped like flowers: a violet was where boats were moored.

On the outskirts of the cities the only open fields were the skies: mechanical skies; chemical skies; mathematical skies, where the signs of the zodiac revolved around each other, each in its own element, but Gemini, the twins, returned more often than the others. The young man got up hurriedly around one o'clock in the morning, convinced that the mirror was leaning forward and about to topple over. He stood it upright with great difficulty and, suddenly worried, decided it was too dangerous to return to his bed, so he sat on a rickety chair, directly in front of the mirror and only one pace away from it.

Then he thought he heard someone else breathing in the room, but no, he was mistaken; there was no one. He then saw a young man standing in front of a huge open door; the young man was totally naked. There was only a black landscape behind him that could have been burnt paper. Only the forms of the objects remained, and it was possible to recognise what those objects had once been and in some cases what substances they had been made from.

Nothing could have been more tragic, really. Some of those things had once belonged to him: jewels, gifts of love, relics of his childhood, and even a small bottle of perfume the cork of which was nowhere to be found. Other items were unknown to him, although he could no doubt determine their original use. The apprentice looked even further into the ashes. He felt a guilty sense of satisfaction when he looked at the smiling young man; his face was like a globe inside which two hummingbirds fluttered. He took the man by the waist and it was, of course, the sides of the mirror that he was holding. And once the birds had flown away, the music rose and followed them in their flight.

What had happened in that room?

Still, since that day the mirror has never been found and I cannot so much as put my lips anywhere near to one of the mirror's possible splinters, even if it means I risk never again seeing those wings of down, those swans about to begin to sing.

www.incunabulamedia.com

SOME OTHER TITLES FROM INCUNABULA

FICTION (mainstream)

Kim Dallesandro
  Trains
  Mad Dog Tag
  Dream Maker
  The Seduction Of Solitude
  Cul De Sac
  Oklahoma
  Reno
  Steam
  The Fragility Of Ice
  The Absurdity Of Abstracts

Travis Michael Holder
  Waiting For Walk

H A Eaglehart
  Urban Native

R J Dent
  Revelation
  Soluble Fish By Andre Breton (Translator)
  The Dead Man & The Solar Anus By Georges Bataille (Translator)

POETRY & ART

Michael McAloran
  Scenes From Nowhere
  ever unto

at the edge of pulse
foreign & unspoken (two plays)
(with D M Mitchell)
ghostmeat
the worse/the better done
cold ash redeem
the once what being

Barton D Smock
wasp, gasp

Matt Leyshon
The Sea Witch
The Witch's Finger

Thomas Schmidt
Sheesh-Capeesh

Ricardo Acevedo
Malo
Night

David Greenslade & David Rees Davies
Perfectly Frank Opens The Door

Donald Brackett & Lance Olsen
Transposed Heads

FANTASY & SURREALISM

Tim Lees
The Ice Plague

D F Lewis
    Gauche Stories
    A Man Too Mean To Be Me

Christian Riley
    Of Woodland Textures and Charnel Delights

Tony Kearns
    Dookie (A Colourful Life)
    Dookie 2 (World War 3)

Simon Whitechapel
    Gweel (And Other Alterities)
    Tales Of Silence & Sortilege

Ian Miller
    The Broken Diary

D M Mitchell
    The Seventh Song of Maldoror
    Split!
    100 Chambers
    The Festival
    In The Black Sun Hotel
    Black Worm Jism

James Havoc
    Satanskin
    White Skull

GHOSTS, DECADENCE AND SYMBOLISM

Lucy Lane Clifford
The New Mother

Various (ed D M Mitchell)
Unfinished Business

H R Wakefield
The Frontier Guards
Farewell Performance

A N L Munby
The Alabaster Hand

John Metcalfe
The Bad Lands

Nugent Barker
Written With My Left Hand

VISIONS (PHOTOGRAPHY)

1. Matt Leyshon
Whereunto The Said Spirit Said They Are The Pictures
2. Syd Howells
Gifts The Dead Left Us
3. Sue Fox
Carnival of the Bizarre
4. Kim Dallesandro
On The Boulevard

Printed and bound by CPI Group (UK) Ltd, Croydon, CR0 4YY
11/03/2024
03734149-0001